TIGER
WOODS

TIGER
WOODS
KING OF THE COURSE

Jeff Savage

Lerner Publications Company ● Minneapolis

On the afternoon that Tiger won the Masters, my son, Taylor Jeffrey Savage, was born. This book is for him.

This book is available in two editions:
Library binding by Lerner Publications Company
Soft cover by First Avenue Editions
241 First Avenue North, Minneapolis, Minnesota 55401

Website address: www.lernerbooks.com

Library of Congress Cataloging-in-Publication Data

Savage, Jeff.
    Tiger Woods : king of the course / Jeff Savage.
      p.   cm.
    Includes bibliographical references and index.
    Summary: A biography of the talented young golfer who won his first U.S. Amateur Championship in 1994 at age 19 and was named Sports Illustrated Sportsman of the Year in 1996.
     ISBN 0–8225–3655–2 (hardcover : alk. paper)
     ISBN 0–8225–9811–6 (softcover : alk. paper)
    1. Woods, Tiger—Juvenile literature. 2. Golfers—United States—Biography—Juvenile literature. [1. Woods, Tiger. 2. Golfers.] I. Title.
GV964.W66S38   1998
796.352'092—dc21
[B]   97–5451

Manufactured in the United States of America
1 2 3 4 5 6 – JR – 04 03 02 01 00 99

Contents

Wearing his lucky red shirt, Tiger tees off during the final round of the 1997 Masters Tournament.

Golf Master

Tiger Woods stood at the 18th tee with his arms folded across his chest. He gazed out at the fairway with a serious look on his small, round, boyish face. Then he reached into his golf bag and pulled out his favorite club. Driver.

Flocks of adoring fans strained against the gallery ropes to praise him. "Attaway, Tiger! You go, T!" they shouted. Tiger gave a shy, toothy grin. Then he tugged on the bill of his cap and concentrated.

Tiger had dreamed of winning the Masters Tournament since he was five years old. He had watched the same tapes over and over again of the fabled contest at Augusta National Golf Club, imagining he would someday be at the final hole with the lead. And on this gentle, cloud-capped Georgia day, Tiger was living his dream. He was winning the 1997 Masters with a bigger lead than anyone in history had ever had. He was ahead by *12 shots.* With one hole to go, he needed a par to break the course record set by the legendary Jack Nicklaus.

With his ball teed up, Tiger drew his club back behind his head and twisted his rubber-band body into a tight coil. Then he unleashed his mighty swing. He swept his muscular arms down and through like steel cables, smacking the ball into a blur that screamed through the air at 180 miles per hour. It sailed far, far into the sky until it was the size of a tiny pea. It landed beyond the farthest fairway **trap** and didn't stop rolling until it was 300 yards away, which is the length of three football fields.

Tiger had left college a few months earlier to join the Professional Golfers' Association Tour. He had already won three PGA tournaments, and people were calling him the best golfer alive. But Tiger had been a teenager not long before, and he was still having fun just being a kid. While the other golfers at Augusta dined on fine food each night following their rounds, Tiger ate burgers and fries with his buddies and played Ping-Pong and video games.

On the course each day, Tiger walked along the ropes exchanging high-fives with fans young and old. They called out his name, and he tossed them golf balls from his bag. He signed hundreds of autographs. Everyone was gripped by the Tiger craze. Weekly passes to the Masters were selling for as much as $10,000.

With a big grin and a laid-back style, Tiger is a fan favorite at any golf course.

More than 50 million people around the world were watching the event on television, making it the most-watched golf tournament ever. Tiger knew his youth and ethnic heritage made him a hero to everyone, especially children and minorities.

Golf has long been a game dominated by whites. The reason is not that black people cannot play the game. It is because in many cases they have not been allowed to. Bigoted members at some clubs have barred minorities from their courses. The founder of the Masters Tournament once said, "As long as I'm alive, golfers will be white, and caddies will be black." Conditions are improving, but as Tiger himself knows, racial prejudice still exists at some golf courses.

Charlie Sifford was the first African American golfer to join the Professional Golfers' Association.

Other African American golfers had competed on the Professional Golfers' Association Tour before Tiger. Charlie Sifford was a pioneer in the 1950s. Calvin Peete, Lee Elder, and Jim Thorpe followed. It was not easy for these men. They were heckled and jeered, and sometimes they even received death threats. When Tiger played in his first pro event, he received a death threat too. Even here in Georgia, no other golfer had a security guard. Tiger had six.

Tiger is one-quarter black, one-quarter Thai, one-quarter Chinese, one-eighth American Indian, and one-eighth white. "But in America," his father, Earl, says, "if you have a drop of black blood in you, you're black." Tiger identifies with all his races. "To say I am just black," he says, "is an injustice to *all* my heritages." Tiger sees himself as simply an American.

Although Tiger is good looking and friendly, he attracts attention mostly for what he can do on the course. A golf course has 18 holes, which vary in length. Each hole ends with a cup, also called a hole. The hole is marked by a flag, and the staff of the flag is known as the pin. A golfer hits the first shot from the tee box. The fairway is the area of grass that stretches from the tee to the green. The cup sits in an area called the green.

Each golfer has a set of clubs that includes at least 3 woods, as many as 10 irons, and a putter. The woods, which have big, rounded clubheads, are generally used off the tee. The 1-wood, which is designed to drive the ball the longest possible distance, is called a driver. Irons are mostly used in the fairway. The putter is used on the green. The object is to use the fewest possible **strokes** to hit the ball into the cup.

The number of strokes a skilled golfer is supposed to take on a hole is called par. Holes are par-3, par-4, or par-5, depending on their length. One stroke less than par is called a birdie. Two strokes less is an eagle. One stroke more than par is a bogey. Two strokes more is a double bogey, and so on. Par for a typical 18-hole course is 72. Shooting better than 72, as Tiger often does, is outstanding.

During the second round of the 1997 Masters, Tiger nabbed the lead, which he held for the rest of the tournament.

On this day of the Masters, Tiger was indeed shooting under par. And he was winning the most honored tournament in golf. In Thursday's chilly air he had shot a nervous 40 on the front nine (first nine holes). No golfer had ever won the tournament with such a poor start. But Tiger fired an amazing 30 on the back nine (last nine holes) to get within three strokes of the leader. Friday he crept closer until, finally, at 5:31 p.m. local time, at the 13th hole, he sank a 20-foot putt for eagle to take the lead. He never let it go. Saturday he moved away from the field with a tournament-best 65 to triple his lead from three strokes to nine. He would never be caught now, and everyone knew it. Sunday's **round** was a parade. Tiger marched from hole to hole as the crowds showered him with applause.

Tiger waved to fans as he walked down the fairway of the 18th hole during the final round of the 1997 Masters.

His fairway shot at the last hole was a **wedge** from 132 yards away. He stood amidst a funnel of fans whose chants of "Tiger—Tiger—Tiger" hushed to silence as he prepared to hit his ball. Slowly, he brought the club up in a **backswing.** Then his hips moved forward and his arms came down and his clubhead moved faster and faster until it was a silver streak of light blasting down into the ball. *Shhwacckkk!* The ball arched through the sky like a rainbow and landed on the green. As Tiger walked to the green in the gathering dusk, the gallery's applause swelled to a loud ovation. Tiger smiled broadly, tipped his cap, and mouthed the words, "Thank you."

Tiger's long putt at the final hole skidded past, and he had to make a tricky five-footer to break Nicklaus's course record of 271. He calmly swept his putter through, and the ball rolled over the velvet green and disappeared into the cup. Cheers rang out as Tiger uppercut the air with his fist and screamed "Yes!" He turned and hugged Fluff Cowan, his caddie, then raised his arms in celebration. At 21, he had become the youngest Masters champion ever, and had broken a number of other records as well.

Applause rained down on Tiger as he greeted his mother and father at the green's edge. Earl bearhugged his son, and Tiger buried his head in his dad's shoulder and wept. Then he reached for his mother, Kultida, squeezed her arm, and cried some more.

Tiger's green sportcoat—which he received after winning the Masters Tournament—was presented to him by Nick Faldo, the winner of the 1996 Masters.

Tiger was the first African American, as well as the first Asian American, to win the Masters. When the ceremonial green jacket was presented to him and he slipped it on, his father smiled and said, "Green and black go well together, don't they?"

When Tiger turned pro, a TV commercial was made in which young faces of every color hit golf shots with tiny clubs, then said to the camera, "I am Tiger Woods." The message was that Tiger is a role model for children. After winning the Masters, Tiger accepted such a role with pride. "I think winning here is going to do a lot for the game of golf," he said. "A lot of kids look up to me just because I'm around their same age group, and they'll start playing golf now. Kids will think golf is cool."

Wielding a pint-sized putter, 11-month-old Tiger
concentrates on tapping a golf ball toward the hole.

16

2

Cub with a Club

Tiger's golf life began in the family garage. He sat in his highchair every day, beginning at six months old, watching his father hit golf balls with a 5-iron into a net. Tiger sat quietly for hours at a time, until the day came when he was able to stand on his own and try his first swing. He gripped his sawed-off putter, set up, wiggled it twice just like his father, and hit the ball. "His first swing was a perfect imitation of mine," Earl said. "It was like looking at myself in a miniature mirror."

Eldrick "Tiger" Woods was born December 30, 1975, to Earl and Kultida Woods. He was their only child. His parents put the first letter of each of their names on both ends of his "to show," Kultida says, "that no matter what, we will always be at your side." His father nicknamed him Tiger after a South Vietnamese soldier who had saved his life from sniper fire.

"It was my hope," Earl says, "that my son would be as courageous as my friend."

Earl was a Green Beret lieutenant colonel in the Vietnam War when he met Kultida in Bangkok, Thailand. She was working as a secretary in a U.S. Army office. They married and moved to Brooklyn, New York, in 1969, and then to Cypress, California, 40 miles south of Los Angeles, where Earl went to work at McDonnell Douglas. Earl had three children from a previous marriage, but none with Kultida. Then Tiger was born.

Earl had played his first round of golf two years earlier. He showed a knack for the game by shooting a respectable 91 his first time out. But he was 42 years old. He had never given much thought to the game when he was younger. "I was a black kid, and golf was played at the country club—end of story," he said. "But I told myself that somehow my son would get a chance to play golf early in life."

As a toddler, Tiger carried his putter wherever he went. "It didn't matter if you picked him up and carried him," says his father, "he'd always hang onto the putter." Tiger swatted at golf balls every day in the garage. Before he was two, his father took him to the Navy Golf Course for the first time. The first hole is 410 yards. Using sawed-off clubs, it took Tiger eight shots to get to the green and three putts to sink the ball in the cup.

At one and a half, Tiger loved whacking a golf ball around the house.

A few months later, Tiger appeared on national television on *The Mike Douglas Show*. Using a golf club taller than he was, he whacked tee shots into a net to the delight of the audience. Then he played against comedian Bob Hope in a putting contest— and won. A year later he appeared on the national television program *That's Incredible!*

By the age of three, Tiger shot a 48 for nine holes. When officials at the Navy course enforced a rule that children under 10 could not play, Earl took his son to nearby Heartwell Park Golf Club. Rudy Duran, the golf pro there, needed only to watch Tiger hit seven shots before approving him to play there. "He had talent oozing out of his fingertips," said Duran.

Tiger—at the age of three—practices driving the ball.

When Tiger was six, his parents gave him a cassette tape that played soft music with a voice that called out messages. The messages were written on pieces of paper and he tacked them to his bookshelf in his tiny bedroom. Some of the messages were: *I focus and give it my all. I believe in me. I smile at obstacles. My strength is great.*

Tiger played the tape over and over again while practicing his swing in front of his bedroom mirror or putting on the carpet. The messages seemed to help his concentration. That year, he got his first hole in one. Then he got his second. On a practice green one day, he sank 80 4-foot putts in a row.

Earl knew life for Tiger would not always be easy in the golf world. Earl had been the first black baseball player in the Big Eight Conference when he played catcher at Kansas State University. Often he was not allowed to stay with his teammates at whites-only hotels, and he sometimes had to eat in parking lots while the rest of the team sat inside the restaurants. Tiger knew it would be difficult too. On his first day of kindergarten, he was tied to a tree and taunted by older white boys.

Tiger was force-fed the mental part of golf. His father would stand 15 feet in front of him and say, "I'm a tree," and Tiger would have to hit wedge shots over him. On the course, Earl would try to distract his son on purpose. He would drop his golf bag during Tiger's backswing. He would roll a ball in front of Tiger just as the boy was about to putt. He would cough and jingle his change and drive the golf cart as Tiger was about to hit the ball. "I wanted to make sure," Earl says, "he'd never run into anybody who was tougher mentally than he was." Tiger understood what his father was doing. "I mean, yeah, I'd get angry sometimes," he says. "But I knew it was for the betterment of me. That's what learning is all about, right?"

Tiger also learned that practice can be fun. His father would challenge him to playful contests, like seeing who could hit the ball closest to the pin while standing on one foot, or who could sink more putts with his eyes closed.

When Tiger was eight, he was 4-foot-6 and weighed 75 pounds, but his drives went 170 yards. He played in his first junior world championship, in the 10-and-under division, at Presidio Park Golf Course in San Diego. At the first tee, where all the boys waited nervously to tee off, his father said, "Son, I want you to know I love you no matter how you do. Enjoy yourself." Tiger smacked a perfect drive down the middle. When the first round ended, Earl asked his son what he had been thinking at the first tee. Tiger simply said, "Where I wanted my ball to go, Daddy." In the final round, Tiger blistered the course with a five under par to win in a breeze. He returned the following year and won again.

Tiger lines up a putt in the Junior World Tournament at
Presidio Park Golf Course in San Diego.

Jack Nicklaus, a top-ranked golfer in the 1960s and 1970s, has 71 PGA victories under his belt. Among these are six Masters Tournament victories, five PGA Championship wins, and four U.S. Open and three British Open wins. Tiger looks up to Nicklaus as being one of the greatest golfers in sports history.

Tiger wouldn't play Little League baseball because it interfered with golf. "I've tried to get him involved with other sports," his father said, "but it's always been golf." Tiger tacked a list of Jack Nicklaus's accomplishments on his bedroom wall to remind himself of the goals he wanted to surpass. He played in as many local junior golf tournaments as he could and soon became known around southern California as the kid with the Coke-bottle glasses and the perfect swing. At the age of 11, he entered more than 30 junior tournaments. He won them all.

Tiger never had a babysitter. Kultida stayed with him always. "I let my husband go," she says. "I stay with Tiger. Tiger is more important than a party." Earl was easy on Tiger. Kultida was not. She punished him when he misbehaved. "No homework," she would say, "no practice." But she didn't mind Earl taking him away to play golf. "At least he will not get hurt in golf," she said.

Kultida would not allow Tiger to whine. She expected him to accept mistakes with grace. He would not grow up spoiled. One time she sat Tiger in front of the television to watch John McEnroe, the tennis star known for his tirades. "See that? Never that," she said, pointing at the TV as McEnroe fussed. "I don't like that. I will not have my reputation as a parent ruined by that."

When Tiger hit a bad shot at a junior tournament once, he smacked his club angrily into his bag. His mother saw him do it. She immediately reported it to the tournament director. Tiger overheard his mother insisting that he be penalized two strokes. "Mom!" he screamed. "Shut up," she said. "Did the club move?

Did the bag move? Who made the bad shot? Whose fault? You want to hit something? Hit yourself in the head."

Tiger continued to win tournaments, and when he turned 12, his name and picture appeared in a magazine. Wally Goodwin saw it. Goodwin was the golf coach at Stanford University, and he wrote Tiger a letter. Tiger was "shocked." He wrote back. His letter impressed the coach. "Perfect grammar, capitals, spelling, punctuation, everything," said Goodwin. Right then, Tiger decided he wanted to go to Stanford. He wasn't even in high school yet.

Earl and Kultida had long agreed that Earl would work until Tiger was old enough to play in national junior tournaments. Then Earl would retire to travel with Tiger, and Kultida would go back to work. That time had come.

Tiger won his third Junior World Tournament at the age of 12. That year he began competing in events across the nation.

As he grew into a teenager, Tiger became known by more and more people as an up-and-coming golf star.

3

Launching a Career

Tiger's life was a scramble. He played in all the national youth tournaments he could. He was in seventh grade, and sometimes he skipped school on Fridays to play. To save money, he and his father flew at night at a cheaper rate, and Tiger squinted in the dull light to do his homework. They would arrive in the morning and head straight for the golf course, where Tiger would play the first round in a red-eyed daze. After a day of golf, they would check into a motel and fall into bed. Tiger didn't win often this way.

One day Tiger said, "Pop, do you think we could get to the site early enough so I could get in a practice round?" His father looked at him and thought for a moment. "Son," he said, "I apologize. I promise you from this day forward, you will have just as good of a chance as any of these country club kids, and if I have to go broke, that's what we're going to do."

Tiger and his father began arriving a day early. They stayed at nice hotels. Tiger played a practice round. And he started winning. He won a tournament in Colorado. He won another in Florida. He won twice in Texas.

By the age of 14, Tiger was surrounded by a host of coaches, together called Team Tiger. John Anselmo was his swing coach. His father was his inspirational coach. And Jay Brunza was his sports psychologist.

In 1990 Tiger won the Junior World Tournament for the fifth time.

Golf is often described as a mental game, testing the mind of the player. As the pressure mounts, players desperately try to stay calm and keep control. As veteran pro Tom Kite says, "Do I have total control? Nah. But neither does anybody else."

Brunza hypnotized Tiger and taught him to concentrate deeply and block out all distractions. Brunza got so good at hypnotizing Tiger he could do it in less than a minute. He could even hypnotize Tiger over the telephone. Eventually, Tiger was able to hypnotize himself on the golf course.

When Tiger entered Western High School in Anaheim, he joined the cross-country team. He quit two weeks later. He liked running, but the cross-country meets interfered with his golf schedule.

In a tournament in Texas that combined PGA Tour pros with junior golfers, Tiger beat or tied 18 of the pros, including his pro playing partner, Tommy Moore. "I wish I could have played like that when I was 14," Moore said after the tournament. "Heck, I wish I could play like that at 27."

When Tiger was 15, a story about him appeared in *Sports Illustrated.* In an interview for the article, Tiger was asked to predict his future. "I plan to get my degree first and then tear up the Tour," he said. "I want to be the best golfer ever."

Tiger's father was not surprised at his son's confidence. "Before," Earl said, "black kids grew up with basketball or football or baseball from the time they could walk. The game became part of them from the beginning. But they always learned golf too late. Not Tiger. Tiger knew how to swing a golf club before he could walk."

Mastering the two parts of golf—the physical part and the mental part—was easy for Tiger. Dealing with racism in the sport was harder. One time Tiger played with his father at a course in Chicago that ordinarily bars blacks, Jews, and women. "People just stared at us," Tiger said. He didn't understand why the color of his skin mattered. "Racism is not your problem, it's theirs," Tiger's mother said. "Just play your game."

Tiger played in the No. 1 spot as a freshman on his high school golf team, but he did not boast about it. He offered tips to anybody who was smart enough to ask for them. Occasionally he missed a match to compete in a bigger tournament—like the day he tried to qualify for the 1991 Nissan Los Angeles Open. Tiger was determined to be the youngest golfer ever to play in a PGA Tournament. He was barely 15 years old.

A certain number of players are allowed to compete in a pro golf tournament. Most are pros who automatically qualify based on their past performances. A few spots are kept open for others. A one-day qualifying tournament is held to determine who gets to enter the actual four-day tournament.

Tiger's dedicated parents do everything possible to help him achieve his golfing ambitions.

Tiger's father drove him in the family Mustang to Los Serranos Country Club in Chino, California, for the one-day qualifying tournament. There were 132 golfers entered. Only two would get spots in the Los Angeles Open. Tiger's father would be his caddie.

Things started badly for Tiger. He hit two cart paths with tee shots, sliced a shot into high rough, and hit a tree. Still, he managed to save par each time. Then, all at once, he caught fire. He holed a 15-foot birdie putt at the 6th and another at the 7th and then chipped in from 40 yards away for an eagle at the 8th. "Don't touch me, I'm burning up," he told his father.

Tiger stood over his second shot at the par-5 18th at six under par. He was 280 yards from a green that was guarded in front by a lake. Other golfers had finished their round, and judging by their scores, it looked like Tiger needed to finish at seven under to make it. He needed a birdie. The safe play would have been a soft iron and a chip. Tiger pulled a wood from his bag. Never mind a birdie, he thought to himself, maybe I can make eagle. Earl agonized over whether to say something. As Tiger studied his shot, Earl spoke up. "Son," he whispered, "you've got to make birdie." Tiger went for the eagle anyway. He reared back and swung hard. The ball zipped low through the air, took one hop, and plunked in the lake. Tiger pulled his cap down over his face. He would get a bogey on the hole, his only one of the day. He watched the Los Angeles Open on TV.

Tiger won his share of tournaments too. He won the Southern California Golf Association High School Invitational as a 10th grader. Then he won the prestigious United States Junior Amateur Championship in a playoff. He was the youngest winner ever. By the time he turned 16, he had won 6 junior world titles against players from around the globe and more than 130 local junior titles. So many trophies filled his bedroom, he could barely get to his bed.

When the Los Angeles Open came to the Riviera Country Club again the following year, Tiger was there—as a player. The Riviera committee had decided that having a fresh young face in its tournament would be good for the game. So the 16-year-old boy was granted an exemption—meaning tournament officials let him play without having to qualify. Tiger was still an amateur, so he wouldn't get to keep any money he won. But Tiger was thrilled just to be playing. Others were not. Committee chairman Mark Kuperstock and Tiger both received death threats from anonymous callers. Several security guards had to walk with Tiger around the course.

At the first tee, on a cliff nearly 100 feet above the fairway, Tiger was frightened. Not of the height, but of being in his first professional tournament. This was his ultimate dream—to play against the pros.

Tiger blasts the ball down the fairway during the Los Angeles Open in 1992.

With nearly 3,000 fans gathered around him, he launched his tee shot off the cliff and down the fairway. And with that shot, Tiger had become the youngest person ever to play on the PGA Tour. Not that he cared about that right now. "I was so tense, I had a tough time holding the club," Tiger said later. "It was like rigor mortis had set in."

On the fairway, Tiger hit another shot that reached the green on the par-5 hole. He sank his second putt for birdie, and on the electronic leader boards all around the golf course, his score was posted: T. WOODS -1. "That," he said afterward, "was neat."

With Earl and Kultida in the gallery, Tiger shot a tidy 72 on that day. But some of the pros didn't know about him yet. When Masters champion Sandy Lyle was asked what he thought of Tiger Woods, Lyle said, "I don't know. I haven't played there yet."

Tiger returned the next day to shoot a 75. He missed the cut by six strokes. He would not get to play on the weekend. When reporters in the press tent asked him if he had learned anything, Tiger smiled and said, "Yes. I learned I'm not that good. But I'll play these guys again—eventually."

4

A Shooting Star

Tiger was obsessed with playing on the PGA Tour. He hardly cared that he won the Junior Amateur Championship again, this time by one stroke. He studied golf records, and he knew that winning junior titles guaranteed nothing. Of the past 44 winners of that championship, only eight had won a single tournament on the PGA Tour.

So why not just turn pro right away? Tennis players were doing so at 14 and younger. Even basketball players were going straight from high school to professional teams. "I'm not mature enough," Tiger admitted. "My body hasn't finished growing and my swing's not good enough yet. The guys on the pro tour don't make dumb decisions. Their thinking is very clear. With me, 16-year-old problems sneak in there every once in a while."

Tiger was a full six feet tall but he weighed just 140 pounds. Being thin as a pencil didn't help his golf game. He tried to gain weight any way he could. He increased his order size at his favorite restaurant— McDonald's. He ate two dinners. He ate midnight snacks. He lifted weights.

One day Tiger's father made a phone call to Butch Harmon in Houston, Texas. Many consider Harmon the Tour's best coach. Earl asked Harmon if he would coach Tiger. Harmon was coaching superstar Greg Norman at the time, but he told Earl he would work with Tiger too.

Coach Harmon shortened Tiger's backswing and tightened up other areas. Tiger could tell the difference immediately. Soon he was calling Harmon every day. "I can't get him off the phone," Harmon said.

To no one's surprise, Tiger won the 1993 Junior Amateur Championship for a record third time. He was two strokes down with two holes left, but he birdied the 17th and the 18th to force a **playoff,** then birdied the first extra hole to win it.

In June of 1993, Tiger struggled through a qualifying round for the U.S. Open. Feeling out of his league and under a lot of pressure, he didn't really want to be there. Tiger's father, who was his caddie, just kept encouraging Tiger. After finishing a round, Tiger fired his father. Although they got over their argument, Earl Woods didn't get his job back.

Tiger and a classmate pose for a yearbook photograph of the two graduating students voted "Most Likely to Succeed."

When Tiger graduated from high school in 1994, he was ready to move on. "Hey, I had a normal childhood," he said. "I studied and went to the mall. I was addicted to TV wrestling, rap music, and *The Simpsons.* I got into trouble and got out of it. I loved my parents and obeyed what they told me." Now Tiger would be leaving home. He had finished high school with a superior grade-point average of 3.79. Colleges around the country had offered him full scholarships. Only one school was ever on Tiger's list—Stanford.

Tiger packed up his belongings, drove north to Palo Alto, and parked amid the eucalyptus trees. Right away he knew he had made the right choice. "I'm not a celebrity at Stanford," he said. "Everybody's special. You have to be to get in here. I'm just lost in a crowd here, which is fine. That's why I love this place." But before Tiger's classes started in late September, he had one last tournament to play—The U.S. Amateur.

Like the Junior Amateur, the U.S. Amateur is played once a year. And like the junior event, the format for the U.S. Amateur is match play. In match play, two golfers go head-to-head. The low scorer on each hole wins that hole. The player who wins the most holes wins the match. Unlike the junior event, which is open to golfers under 18, the U.S. Amateur is open to golfers of any age. The competition is fierce.

Tiger looks on in anticipation as his ball rolls toward the hole during the 1994 U.S. Amateur.

The 1994 tournament was held amid the lagoons and railroad ties of the Stadium course at the TPC-Sawgrass in Ponte Vedra, Florida. A PGA Tournament is also held each year on the course, and Tiger had watched it many times on television. He remembered that the 17th was the famous Island Green hole, which is surrounded by water. And it was on this very hole, on the first day, that Tiger won his first match. He was one up on 46-year-old Vaughn Moise of Texas when they arrived at the 17th. The wind was blowing and Moise hit his tee shot into the black swamp water. With a 9-iron, Tiger smartly lofted the ball to the green and two-putted for par to win the match and advance to the field of 32.

In the second round, Tiger faced Buddy Alexander, the 41-year-old golf coach at the University of Florida who had won the Amateur once already. After eight holes, Tiger trailed by four. But he came storming back to square the match after 16. Once again, Tiger stood with his opponent at the famous 17th. The wind was blowing harder than the day before. Tiger went first. He drew back his 9-iron and swung. His shot started toward the hole, but the wind began to carry it left toward the swamp water. Tiger leaned right. His caddie leaned right. The ball landed on the green and rolled toward the water. It stopped eight inches from the edge. "I was about to pass out," said Tiger, who went on to win the match.

Tiger beat his next three opponents to reach the final match. By doing so, he qualified for the Masters Tournament in April. But he didn't want to think about that now. He wanted to win the Amateur. His opponent in the 36-hole final match was Trip Kuehne, a junior at Oklahoma State University. If Tiger could win, he would become the youngest winner, the first black winner, and first to win both the Amateur and the Junior Amateur, which he had won a record three times. He also would qualify for the next U.S. Open and British Open. Pressure? Well, maybe a little. As Tiger left the clubhouse to start the match, his father whispered in his ear, "Let the legend grow."

Instead, Tiger fell behind early. Kuehne birdied seven of the first 13 holes and was up six. At the lunch break, with 18 holes left, he was still up four. But once again, Tiger clawed his way back. He cut the lead to three, then two, then one, and then he pulled even at the 16th with a 5-foot birdie putt. And once more, Tiger stood side-by-side with his opponent at the 17th.

Tiger went first. He selected a 9-iron. But just as he was about to hit, the wind changed. So did he. He went to his bag and exchanged his 9-iron for a pitching wedge. It was a bold move. The hole was 139 yards away, and anything short would splash into the water. Tiger adjusted his straw hat and stepped up to the ball. He drew his club back and swung down hard. The ball sailed over the black swamp water, caught the **fringe,** spun back, and stopped at the green's edge, just inches from the water. Kultida was watching on television at home in Cypress, and she fell off the bed onto the floor when the ball landed. "That boy almost gave me a heart attack," she said. "That boy tried to kill me."

Kuehne smacked his shot to the middle of the green, but it didn't matter. Tiger calmly sank his 14-foot birdie putt to take the lead, and he punched the air in celebration. When Kuehne missed his par putt at the 18th, it was over. Earl dropped his walking stick and charged onto the green, where he and Tiger hugged and cried. It was the greatest comeback in the 99-year history of the Amateur. "What an amazing feeling this is," Tiger said. "It feels great to be a champion. It's just indescribable."

When Tiger returned to Stanford to start classes, he was congratulated by fellow students and quizzed on how long he would stay in school. Phil Mickelson, the last great collegiate golfer, had recently signed a $5 million, five-year deal with a sporting goods manufacturer. People were saying Tiger was worth even more. Five-time British Open champion Tom Watson went so far as to call Tiger, "potentially the most important player to enter the game in 50 years." Tiger appreciated the attention, but he had no intention of leaving Stanford. After all, he had just gotten there.

On to the Tour

When Tiger met his Stanford golf teammates, he realized he was in pretty good company. The four of them had won the NCAA team championship the year before—without him. He was the newcomer. And in fun, they treated him like it. They made him carry the extra luggage on road trips. They made him sit in the front of the van—next to the coach. They teased him often. And they cherished his ability to play golf.

Tiger may have been just a freshman, but he didn't play like one. He won his first college event. By the season's midpoint, he was the No. 1–ranked collegiate player in the country.

In the spring of 1995, the Stanford team took a trip to the dreaded Shoal Creek Country Club outside Birmingham, Alabama. When the PGA Championship was played at Shoal Creek five years earlier, club founder Hall Thompson told reporters that members of his club "don't discriminate in every other area except the blacks." Tiger knew the ugly history of Shoal Creek. He wanted to go anyway.

"What a great slap in the face it would be to those who think minorities are inferior," said Tiger's teammate, Notah Begay, "if he went down and won." When a reporter asked Tiger if racist policies at certain country clubs inspired him to try harder, he said no. His father chuckled at his answer. "Of course it does," Earl said.

During the tournament, black employees at the country club sneaked up to Tiger and whispered encouragement in his ear. Maybe it helped. Tied for the lead at the par-5 17th, he blasted a driver and a 3-wood to reach the end of the fairway in two shots. He rolled a 50-foot putt to the hole and tapped in for birdie and the lead. At the 18th, with Hall Thompson standing over his shoulder, Tiger unleashed a towering drive down the middle. Then he smacked a 7-iron to the green, and knocked in his 20-footer for another birdie, winning by two. He boarded a plane with his teammates for home and fell asleep. The smile on his lips stayed.

Tiger was nervous in the days leading up to the 1995 Masters Tournament in Augusta, Georgia. The world's four greatest golf tournaments are the Masters, the U.S. Open, the British Open, and the PGA

Championship, together called the Grand Slam. The Masters is considered the best of the four. To play in it is every golfer's dream. The greens at Augusta National Golf Club are as smooth as glass, so Tiger practiced his putting on the basketball floor at Stanford's Maples Pavilion. He knew his chances of winning were near impossible—no amateur had ever won—but he didn't want to embarrass himself either. "To walk where Bobby Jones and Jack Nicklaus walked, that will be daunting," he said. "But I'm not afraid of the Masters. I'm not afraid of anything."

Tiger signs autographs for young fans at Augusta National Golf Club, where he was playing in the 1995 Masters Tournament.

Tiger stepped out in front of a huge gallery on the first tee at Augusta—exactly 20 years after Lee Elder broke the color barrier there. It was an important moment for Tiger and for his father. When Tiger's name was announced, his father nearly cried. Then, under a light sprinkle of rain, Tiger cracked his first drive down the middle.

On the first green, Tiger sized up his 40-foot birdie putt, then lightly tapped the ball with his putter. The ball rolled slowly toward the hole and right on by. It went clear off the green. Tiger was discovering Augusta. After a 1st-hole bogey, Tiger blasted his second tee shot into some tall pines. His playing partner, defending champion Jose Maria Olazabal, figured Tiger was in for a long and difficult afternoon. But Olazabal did not know Tiger any better than Tiger knew Augusta.

Tiger grabbed his 3-iron and slashed his ball off a clump of pine needles 235 yards to the green. He sank a birdie putt and was even again. He finished the day that way.

Tiger shot even—a par 72—again the next day. "I feel happy to make the cut," he said. "I'm having the time of my life." On Saturday, he sagged with a 77, but he returned Sunday with another 72 to finish the tournament at five over par. His cool temperament had impressed the pros. "He might be ready to win the Masters right now," said Greg Norman.

During the 1995 Masters Tournament, Tiger's caddie at Augusta helps him line up a putt on the 17th green.

Tiger packed his belongings and hurried back to Stanford, where he had a history class the next morning. Before leaving, though, he wrote a letter of appreciation to Masters officials. It read, in part:

Please accept my sincere thanks for providing me the opportunity to experience the most wonderful week of my life. It was fantasy land and Disney World wrapped into one . . . It is here that I left my youth behind and became a man.
Sincerely,
Tiger Woods

Tiger didn't have nearly the fun in his next big tournament two months later—the U.S. Open. At the Shinnecock Hills Golf Club in Southampton, Rhode Island, Tiger thrilled the crowd the first day by routinely out-driving his playing partners, Ernie Els and Nick Price, by 50 yards or more. But Tiger finished with a 74. The next day at the 3rd hole, he injured his wrist swinging a wedge in the high, thick grass. He had to withdraw.

Later that summer, the 1995 U.S. Amateur was staged at Newport, Rhode Island. Tiger's wrist had recovered in time for him to defend his title, and he won again, this time coming from three down to beat Buddy Marucci in the final. "This one means more to me," he said afterward, "because it shows how far my game has come."

Tiger gets a bear hug from his father after winning his second U.S. Amateur Tournament.

A month later at the British Open, Tiger marveled at the way pros like Fred Couples, Greg Norman, and Nick Faldo hit the ball. After missing the cut he asked his coach, Butch Harmon, "Butch, how far away am I? When will I be that good?" Harmon leveled with his teenage student. "Tiger, you just have to keep working," he said. "You've got so much to learn."

Playing as a member of the Stanford University golf team, Tiger chips the ball onto the 6th green during the 1996 NCAA Men's Golf Championship in Ooltewah, Tennessee.

Tiger spent a good part of his sophomore year at Stanford in the weight room. He lifted weights for more than an hour each day, and did another hour of aerobics and stretching. He packed 10 pounds of muscle on to his frame and won almost every collegiate tournament he entered, shattering several course records along the way. He won the Pac-10 championships, the NCAA West Regional, and the NCAA championships.

At the U.S. Open in June 1996, Tiger actually had the lead in the first round. On the Oakland Hills Country Club in Michigan, Tiger birdied the 5th, the 6th, and the 12th, and his name went to the top of the leader board. No amateur had won the Open since 1933. But Tiger could not hold on. He got a horrifying quadruple bogey at the 16th when he hit into the greenside pond—twice. "Unfortunately," he said, "my swing kind of left me a little bit." But Tiger showed his spirit by coming back the next day with a 69. And the dreaded greenside pond hole? He birdied it.

At the British Open in July, he finished 22nd, in the middle of the pack. He was keeping up now with the best players in the world. Even the top pros were advising him to turn pro. "The quicker he gets out here," Curtis Strange said, "the quicker he gets to be the best player in the world."

A month later, in another dramatic U.S. Amateur final, Tiger made history. At Pumpkin Ridge near

Portland, Oregon, he was five under par with 16 holes left. He was still two down with three holes to go. He beat Steve Scott on the second playoff hole to win a record-breaking third straight title. "This is by far the best," he said. "By far." Tiger knew then that it was time to turn pro.

On Wednesday, August 28, 1996, he leaned into a microphone in front of a room filled with media and said two words: "Hello, world." That day he signed deals to endorse Nike and Titleist products in exchange for a whopping $60 million.

The next day he teed up his first professional golf ball at the Greater Milwaukee Open in Wisconsin. What about college? "I made a commitment to get my degree [in economics]," Tiger said, "and I will keep it."

At the tournament in Milwaukee, teens screamed his name so loud and for so long that he had to wave from his hotel window to get them to calm down. "It was like he was the Pope," said Kultida. By week's end, he was clearly drained and it showed in his game. He finished 60th. He did shoot a hole in one though. He took the ball out of the hole and tossed it to a child as a souvenir.

The fall of 1996, a Nike commercial on TV showed Tiger saying: "There are still golf courses in the United States that I cannot play because of the color of my skin. I'm told I'm not ready for you. Are you ready for me?"

Coming from behind, Tiger celebrates after tying the match on the 35th hole at the 1996 U.S. Amateur Tournament.

Fans were indeed ready for him. The PGA Tour pros weren't. He came closer to winning in his second tournament with an 11th-place finish, and then closer still with a 6th-place finish at the Canadian Open in Ontario. He was improving each week.

At the Quad City Classic in Coal Valley, Illinois, they had to print more tickets when they announced he was coming. This time he had the lead on the final day, before four-putting a hole and finishing third.

And then Tiger reached his goal. He won the Las Vegas Invitational by beating Davis Love III on the first hole of a playoff. "He's just so cool," one 12-year-old boy said. "It's really neat that someone his age can beat everybody." Tiger's jackpot was $297,000. He didn't care much about the money. After all, he had just signed deals for $60 million. Tiger cared about winning.

In Texas the next week, with thousands of Tiger tailers chasing him along the ropes and squealing his name, he finished third. A week later in Orlando, he won again. Then Tiger overcame a dreadful cold to win the Walt Disney World/Oldsmobile Classic by two strokes. "If this is how he is every week, then it's over," veteran pro Peter Jacobsen muttered. "He's the greatest player in the history of the game." In the first tournament of 1997—the Mercedes Championships in San Diego—he won for the third time. "At last," the immortal Jack Nicklaus declared. "We have somebody to dominate now."

Three months later, nearly 50 years to the day after Jackie Robinson became the first African American to play major league baseball, Tiger became the first minority golfer to win the famed Masters Tournament.

Tiger jokes with his coach, Butch Harmon, at the 1997
Mercedes Championships in Carlsbad, California.

Back in 1975, the year Tiger was born, Lee Elder was
the first black man to compete in the Masters. Elder
returned to Augusta National 22 years later to watch
Tiger play, and he said before the final round, "If
Tiger Woods wins here, it might have more potential
than Jackie Robinson's break into baseball." After
Tiger won, he spotted Elder standing alone near a
practice green. He approached Elder and whispered
in his ear, "Thanks for making this possible." Elder
stood quietly with tears in his eyes.

As Norman Baker, a New York professor of history,
puts it, "If you hand-picked someone to break barri-
ers, if you created a model, Tiger Woods fits. He is
the modern Jackie Robinson."

Tiger understands his place in history. He knows
what he represents to millions of people. He is proud
of his black heritage, yet he is proud of all his heritages. He will continue to recite a phrase he has re-
peated a hundred times: "I don't want to be the best
black golfer ever. I want to be the best golfer ever."

Career Highlights

- Won first junior world tournament at age 8, San Diego, California, 1984
- Won all 30 junior tournaments entered at age 11, 1987
- Won United States Junior Amateur Championship, 1991, 1992, 1993
- Won United States Amateur Championship, 1994, 1995, 1996
- Played as amateur in first PGA Tour event at age 16, Los Angeles, California, 1992
- Played as amateur in first Masters, United States Open, and British Open at age 19, 1995
- Won NCAA Individual Chamionships, 1995
- Turned professional, 28 August 1996
- Won first PGA Tour event, Las Vegas, Nevada, 1996
- Won second PGA tour event, Orlando, Florida, 1996
- Named Sports Illustrated Sportsman of the Year, 1996
- Won third PGA Tour event, San Diego, California, 1997
- Won Masters Tournament, Augusta, Georgia, 1997

Glossary

backswing: The motion of the golfer and club that brings the club up and away from the ball before making the swing forward.

fringe: A border around the green where the grass is slightly longer than that on the green.

playoff: Additional play at the end of a competition in which players are tied. In match play, a tie at the end of competition requires the players to go on until a player wins a hole, thereby winning the match. In stroke play, tied golfers continue to play until one of them scores lower than the other on a playoff hole.

round: A complete game of golf (18 holes).

stroke: A swing, or attempt to hit the golf ball.

trap: A trap (or sand trap) is a bunker, or depression in the ground, containing sand. Sand traps and other obstacles on a golf course are called hazards.

wedge: An iron designed to chip the ball, giving it height without a lot of distance.

Sources

Information for this book was obtained from the following sources: Dave Anderson (*The New York Times*, 7 April 1995, 14 June 1996); The Associated Press, 30 May 1996, 20 October 1996; Jeff Babineau (*Orlando Sentinel*, 21 October 1996); Thomas Boswell (*Golf Magazine*, December 1995); Bill Brink (*The New York Times*, 16 June 1995); Tim Crothers (*Sports Illustrated*, 25 March 1991); Peter de Jonge (*The New York Times*, 5 February 1995); Jaime Diaz (*The New York Times*, 2 August 1992, 2 September 1996); Larry Dorman (*The New York Times*, 26 August 1994, 29 August 1994, 31 August 1994, 4 April 1995, 8 April 1995); *Ebony*, May 1995; John Garrity (*Sports Illustrated*, 24 February 1992); Bob Harig (*St. Petersburg Times*, 14 April 1997); Bruce Jenkins (*San Francisco Chronicle*, 11 April 1996); Curry Kirkpatrick (*Newsweek*, 10 April 1995); Mark Kriedler (*Sacramento Bee*, 31 August 1996); Joe Logan (Knight-Ridder Newspapers, 26 August 1996); Leigh Montville (*Sports Illustrated*, 9 September 1996); Scott Ostler (*San Francisco Chronicle*, 6 September 1996); *People Weekly*, 23 September 1991, 26 December 1994); Jerry Potter (*USA TODAY*, 7 October 1996); Rick Reilly (*Sports Illustrated*, 27 March 1995, 21 April 1997); Reuters, 10 April 1995; Tim Rosaforte (*Sports Illustrated*, 5 September 1994, 4 September 1995); Geoff Russell (*The New York Times*, 28 August 1995); Tom Shanahan (*San Diego Tribune*, 16 July 1986); Leonard Shapiro (*Washington Post*, 14 April 1997); Pat Sullivan (*San Francisco Chronicle*, 14 June 1996); *The New York Times*, 17 June 1995); and Mike Wise (*The New York Times*, 2 October 1994).

Index

Write to Tiger:

You can send mail to Tiger at the address on the right. If you write a letter, don't get your hopes up too high. Tiger and other athletes get lots of letters every day, and they aren't always able to answer them all.

Mr. Tiger Woods
International Management Group
1 Erieview Plaza, Suite 300
Cleveland, Ohio 44114

Acknowledgments

Photographs are reproduced with the permission of: pp. 1, 6, 9, 10, 12, 13, 15, 24, 36, 38, 46, 53, 54, 57, 58, 59, AP/Wide World Photos; p. 2, Robert Beck/*Sports Illustrated*/© Time Inc.; pp. 16, 19, 20, © David Strick/Outline; p. 23, *San Diego Union-Tribune*/Dave Siccardi; p. 27, *San Diego Union-Tribune*/Joe Flynn; p. 28, © ALLSPORT USA/Alan Levenson; p. 30, *San Diego Union-Tribune*/Lillian Kossacoff; p. 33, © ALLSPORT USA/Ken Levine; p. 41, Seth Poppel Yearbook Archives; p. 42, © ALLSPORT USA/Rusty Jarrett; p. 49, Jacqueline Duvoisin/*Sports Illustrated*/© Time Inc.; p. 51, © ALLSPORT USA/David Cannon.

Front cover photograph and back cover photograph by AP/Wide World Photos.

Artwork by John Erste.

About the Author

Jeff Savage was born in Oakland, California, and grew up in nearby Fremont. He graduated from the University of California at San Diego in 1988 with a degree in journalism and worked as a sportswriter for eight years at the San Diego Union-Tribune. He is the author of more than 30 books for young readers. In addition to his work as a writer, Jeff plays golf, practices karate, and flies airplanes. He lives with his wife, Nancy, and son, Taylor, in Napa, California.